Together

Together

Hazel Hutchins
Art by Alice Priestley

annick press
toronto + new york + vancouver

What keeps my shirt together,
happy over my tummy?

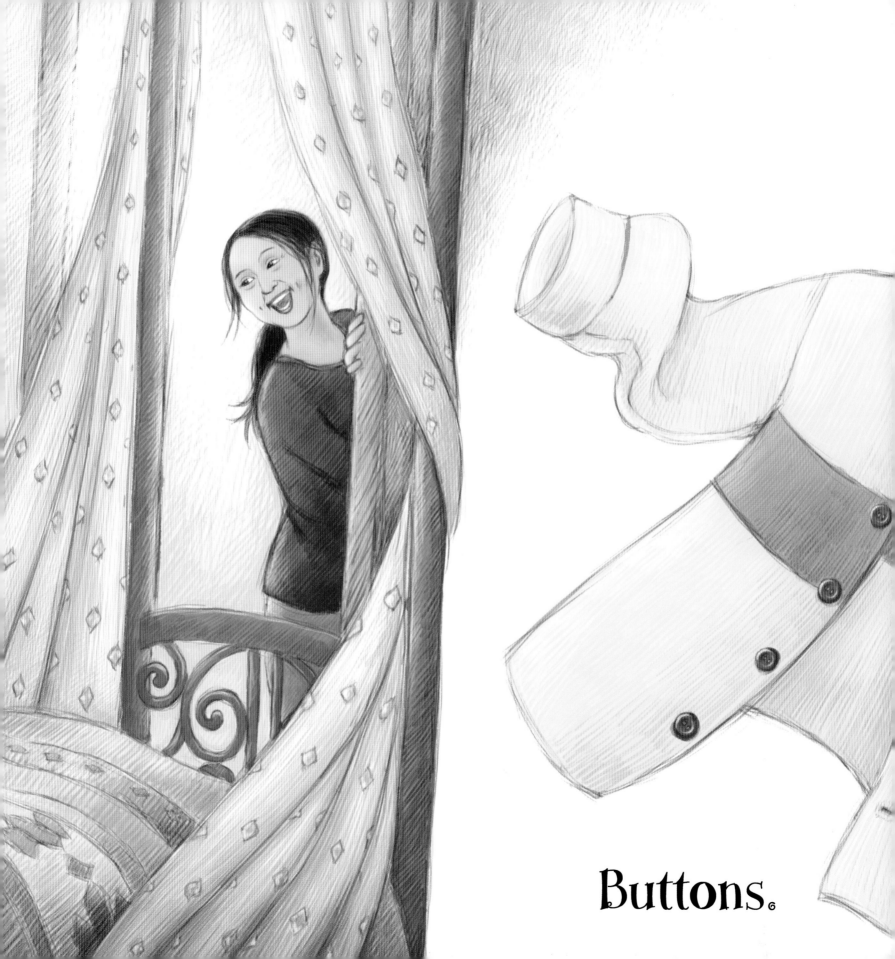

Buttons.

What keeps my pants fastened safe around my waist?

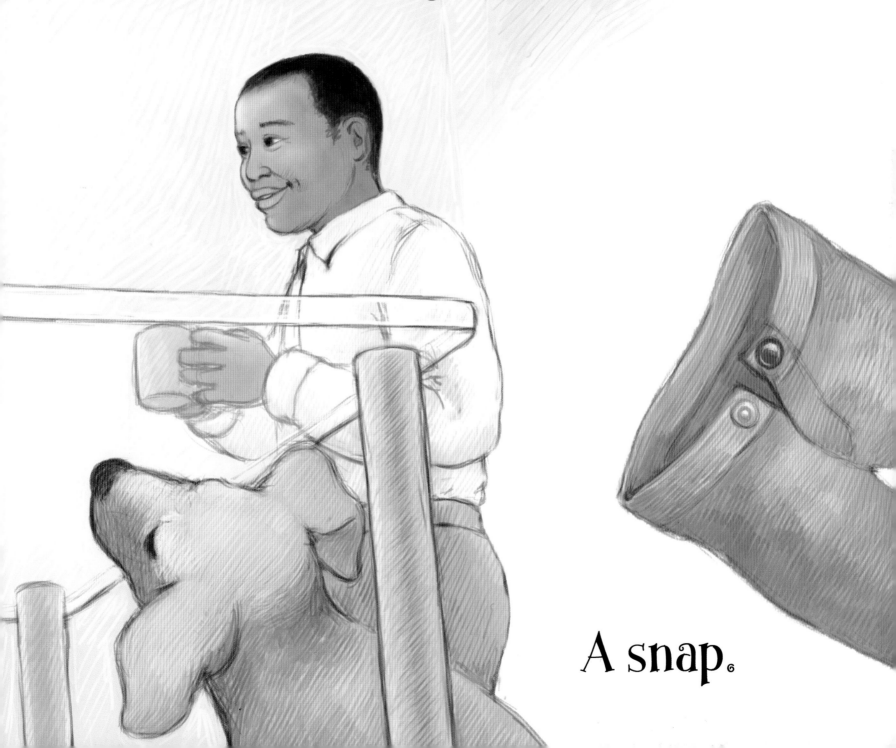

A snap.

What keeps my hair crissy-cross in its braid?

An elastic.

What keeps
my feet from
dancing out
of my shoes?

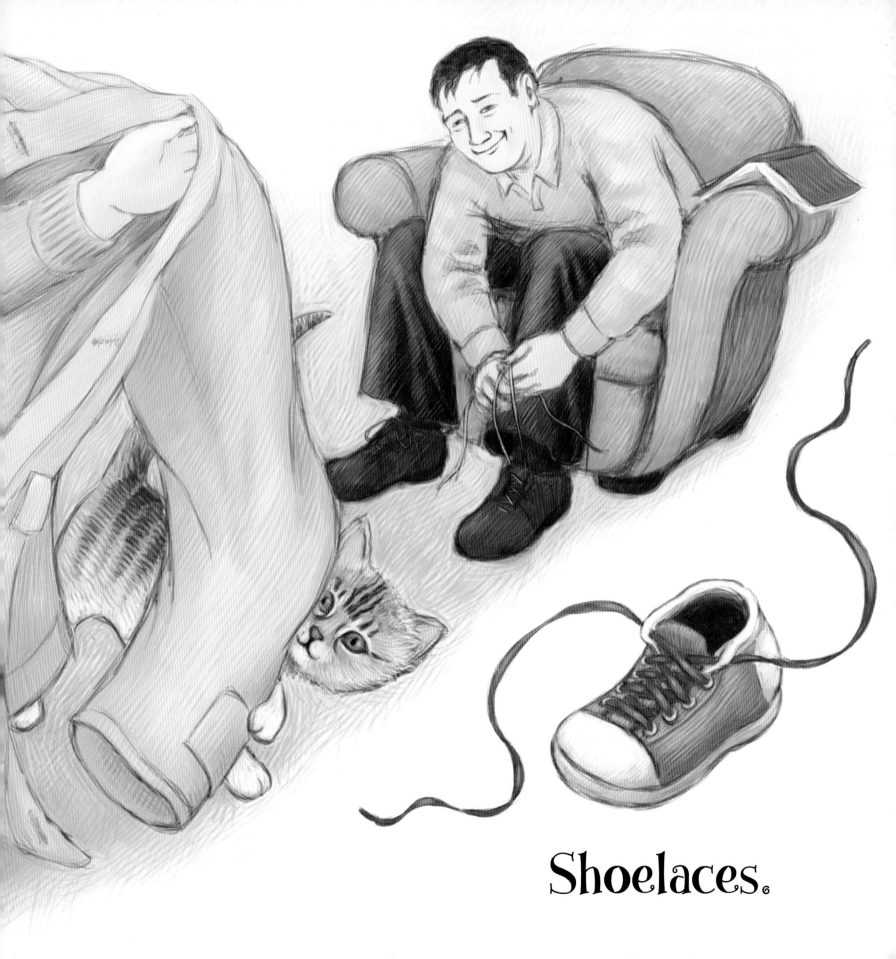

Shoelaces.

What keeps my coat close
and snug all over?

A zipper.

What keeps my snack in my backpack when I run?

A clip.

What keeps my hat from sailing off with the wind?

Velcro.

What keeps my family together when we're apart?

A hug.
One when we leave ...

and one when we're
all back together again.

©2009 Hazel Hutchins (text)
©2009 Alice Priestley (art)
Design: Sheryl Shapiro and Alice Priestley

Annick Press Ltd.

We acknowledge the support of the Canada Council for the Arts, the Ontario Arts Council, and the Government of Canada through the Book Publishing Industry Development Program (BPIDP) for our publishing activities.

ONTARIO ARTS COUNCIL
CONSEIL DES ARTS DE L'ONTARIO

Cataloging in Publication

Hutchins, H. J. (Hazel J.)
        Together / by Hazel Hutchins ; illustrated by Alice Priestley.

ISBN 978-1-55451-208-9 (bound).—ISBN 978-1-55451-207-2 (pbk.)

        I. Priestley, Alice II. Title.

PS8565.U826T65 2009   jC813'.54   C2009-903075-6

The art in this book was rendered digitally.
The text was typeset in Fiddlestix.

Distributed in Canada by:
Firefly Books Ltd.
66 Leek Crescent
Richmond Hill, ON
L4B 1H1

Published in the U.S.A. by:
Annick Press (U.S.) Ltd.
Distributed in the U.S.A. by:
Firefly Books (U.S.) Inc.
P.O. Box 1338
Ellicott Station
Buffalo, NY 14205

Printed in China.

Visit Annick at: www.annickpress.com
Visit Hazel Hutchins at: www.telusplanet.net/public/hjhutch
Visit Alice Priestley at: www.alicepriestley.com

For Isaac
—H.H.

To all my cousins and all their kids
—A.P.